Goodnight Peppa

Once upon a time, Granny and Grandpa Pig came round for dinner. It was almost time for Peppa and George to go to bed.

"YAWN!" yawned Daddy Pig, very loudly, while they were eating.
"Hee! Hee! Hee!" everyone giggled.
"Ho! Ho! Ho! Sorry," snorted Daddy Pig.
"I'm a little tired!"

Peppa and George weren't tired at all.
"Can we jump in puddles for just a tiny bit?" asked Peppa.

"Pleeaassse!"

"OK," said Daddy Pig.
"But you must come in at bath time."

Squelch! Squelch! Squelch!

Peppa and George loved jumping in muddy puddles.
They jumped up and down until they were covered in mud.
"Peppa! George!" called Daddy Pig. "You must be feeling sleepy
after all that jumping. Let's get you in the bath."
"But, Daddy. We are not even a little bit sleepy!" replied Peppa.

Peppa and George splashed in the bath until they were both nice and clean.

Splash! Splash! Splash!

"I think bath time is over," said Daddy Pig, dripping wet.
"You must be tired after all that splashing."

"We're not even a little bit tired!"
cried Peppa, splashing Daddy Pig again.
"Snort! Snort!" laughed George.
Daddy Pig was soaked!

Peppa and George hopped out of the bath . . .

They dried off and put their pyjamas on **very** slowly . . .

Then they brushed their teeth for an extra long time.
Brush! Brush! Brush!
"Quick, wash your faces. Granny Pig wants to tuck you into bed," said Mummy Pig.
"Yippee!" cheered Peppa.
"Gangy-ig!" cheered George.

Peppa and George were **finally** ready for bed. They said goodnight to Mummy and Daddy Pig, and found Granny Pig in their room. "Come on, little ones," said Granny Pig. "It's bedtime. Hop in." "I can't go to bed without Teddy," said Peppa. "Dine-saw!" sobbed George.

So Granny Pig found Teddy and Mr Dinosaur,
and tucked everyone in.
"Goodnight, Peppa and Teddy," said Granny Pig.
"Goodnight, George and Mr Dinosaur."
"But we are not even the tiniest bit sleepy,
Granny," said Peppa.

"I see," said Granny Pig. "I wonder what will make you sleepy?"
"Can you tell us a bedtime story?" asked Peppa.
"Of course, Peppa," replied Granny Pig. "As long as you promise to go to sleep as soon as the story ends."
"We promise!" cried Peppa.

Peppa and George loved bedtime stories.

Granny Pig began telling a story. "Once upon a time, there was –"
"A beautiful princess called Peppa," interrupted Peppa.
"Yes," said Granny Pig. "And –"

Hee! Hee!

"Sir George the brave knight!" Peppa interrupted again.
"Hee! Hee!" giggled George.
Granny Pig carried on. "Princess Peppa and Sir George
lived in a castle –"

"A great big castle in the sky," said Peppa.
Granny Pig tried to finish the story. "Princess Peppa and Sir George had been playing all day in the castle and were very tired –"

"Then the king arrived!" cheered Peppa. "And a cook, and a wizard, and a scary dragon dinosaur!"
"Dine-saw!" added George. "Grrr!"

"And the cook made them all a giant picnic with sandwiches, cakes, jelly . . ." Peppa listed all the foods she could think of.

Grandpa Pig came to find Granny Pig.
"I'm telling Peppa and George a bedtime story," explained Granny Pig.
"And we promised to go to sleep when the story ends," added Peppa.

"I see," said Grandpa Pig. "Granny Pig, why don't you leave this to me? I'm good at ending stories."
So Granny Pig said goodnight and went downstairs.

Grandpa Pig did his best to end the story.
"After they ate the lovely picnic . . . everyone fell asleep!
The end."
But Peppa did not want the story to end.

"Then they all woke up and their friends arrived!"
she cried. "And they went for a ride in Princess Peppa's
carriage and decided to have a great big party!"

Soon, Daddy Pig came upstairs.

"I'm the expert at telling bedtime stories," he said.
Then he whispered quietly to Grandpa Pig, "I'll have
them asleep in no time."
So Grandpa Pig said goodnight and went downstairs.

"Princess Peppa and Sir George were just about to have a great **big** party!" Peppa told Daddy Pig.
"I see," he replied.

Thud! Thud! Thud!

Mummy Pig heard banging, so she came upstairs, too.
Peppa, George and Daddy Pig were dancing!
"We're having a party like in the story!" explained Peppa.

"They're almost asleep!" said Daddy Pig.
"Thank you, Daddy," said Mummy Pig.
"I'll take over now."
So Daddy Pig said goodnight and
went downstairs.

Mummy Pig tucked Peppa and George back into bed. Then she asked Peppa to tell her the whole bedtime story from the beginning, very quietly . . .

"Once upon a time," whispered Peppa, yawning, "there was a beautiful princess called Peppa."

"She lived with Sir George the brave knight in a great big castle in the . . . YAWN . . . sky . . ."
Speaking softly was making Peppa **really** sleepy.

Peppa tried to finish the story, but she just couldn't keep her eyes open. Soon George fell fast asleep, and so did Peppa.

Mummy Pig looked at her two little ones, smiled and whispered, "Goodnight, George. Goodnight, Peppa." Then she headed downstairs to find Granny, Grandpa and Daddy Pig . . .

Snore

Snore
Snore

They were all **fast** asleep!
It was bedtime for Peppa and George,
and it was bedtime for everyone else, too!
"Goodnight!" said Mummy Pig.